SAM ™
THE ANT

THE FLOOD
La Inundación

Follow Your Curiosity at www.SamTheAnt.com
for Children's Books, Brainwave Games, and Music!

samtheantofficial@gmail.com

@samdantofficial

Book #1
Created & Written By Sam Feldman & Enrique C. Feldman
Illustrated By Abraham Mendoza

To all the parents and their children, to all the smiles, hugs, and dreams which they share. To the dreamers: to all the dreams that were and that will be. To the everlasting creative spirit burning inside every dreamer. Keep dreaming, creating... exploring.

Thank you Nick Feldman for your love, belief and inspiration as these stories were created. You embody many of the positive traits found in all of these books.

Sam the ant was a curious ant, who loved to explore the world and find new things. Sam was doing just that when, suddenly, a drop of water fell on the ground.

La hormiga Sam era una hormiga curiosa, a quien le gustaba explorar el mundo y encontrar cosas nuevas. Sam estaba haciendo precisamente eso, cuando de repente, una gota de agua cayó en el suelo.

"Where does water come from?"

¿De dónde viene el agua?

Sam's best friend, Sandy the ant, was curious too, and loved to go out exploring with Sam. They both noticed two more drops of water that hit the ground.

El mejor amigo de Sam, la hormiga Sandy, era curioso también, y le gustaba salir a explorar con Sam. Los dos notaron dos gotas más de agua que golpearon el suelo.

"What is friendship?"

¿Qué es la amistad?

Two drops of water turned into 10 and then... a storm! What used to be dry patches of ground became rivers of raging water!

Dos gotas de agua se convirtieron en 10 y luego ... una tormenta! Lo que eran áreas de tierra seca se convirtieron en ríos de aguas bravas!

"How many water drops have fallen so far?"

"¿Cuántas gotas de agua han caído hasta ahora?"

Sam and Sandy saw a large leaf floating by and Sam pulled Sandy onto the leaf, using it like a boat.

Sam y Sandy vieron una hoja grande flotando y Sam sacó Sandy a la hoja, usando la hoja como un barco.

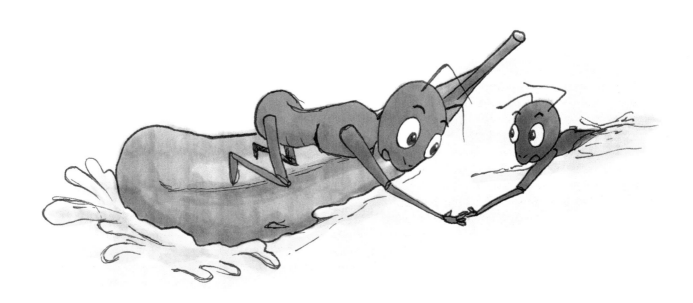

"How is a leaf like a boat? How is it different?"

"¿De que forma es una hoja como un barco? ¿Cómo es diferente?"

They sailed down the raging river. The storm became stronger, and more rain came down than either Sam or Sandy had ever seen. "Don't worry Sandy, we'll find a way to safety!" said Sam.

Navegaban por el río embravecido! La tormenta se puso más fuerte, y más lluvia cayó que lo que Sam o Sandy habían visto en su vida. "No se preocupe Sandy, vamos a encontrar una manera de llegar a la seguridad!", dijo Sam.

"What should they do next?"

"¿Qué deben hacer ahora?"

The leaf boat tossed from side to side and then it bumped into a large rock. THUMP! Sam and Sandy fell into the raging river and clung onto the rock, feeling very far from safety.

El barco de la hoja tiró de lado a lado y luego se topó con una roca grande. ¡THUMP! Sam y Sandy cayeron en el río bravo, aferrándose a la roca, sintiendo muy lejos de seguridad.

Sam heard a buzzing sound, looked up, and saw a flying animal in the air hurling towards them. Sandy shrieked, "What's that?!" Sam and Sandy were scared. They had never seen anything so different before.

Sam escuchó un sonido de zumbido, alzó la vista y vio a un animal volando en el aire lanzando hacia ellos. Sandy gritó, "¿Qué es eso?!" Sam y Sandy tenían miedo. Nunca habían visto algo tan diferente.

The flying animal landed on the rock and said, "Climb onto my back and I'll fly you to higher ground!"

El animal volador aterrizó en la roca y dijo, "Subense a mi espalda y los voy a volar a tierra más alta!"

"Is the flying animal an insect? Are Sam and Sandy insects?"

"¿Es el animal volador un insecto? ¿Son insectos Sam y Sandy?"

Sandy looked nervous. Sam was also worried, but knew they needed help. "What are you?" Sam said.

Sandy parecía nervioso. Sam también estaba preocupado, pero sabía que necesitaba ayuda. "¿Qué es usted?", dijo Sam.

"It's more important to know who I am and how I can help you. I'm Drag, and I know how to fly!"

"Es más importante saber quién soy y cómo los puedo ayudar. Soy Drag, y sé cómo volar!"

"Should they fly to higher ground?"

"¿Deben de volar a tierra más alta?"

Sandy looked very worried and whispered, "How do we know we can trust this thing? We've never seen one before. It might eat us!"

Sandy parecía muy preocupada y le susurró: "¿Cómo sabemos que podemos confiar en esta cosa? Nunca hemos visto nada asi. Nos podría comer!"

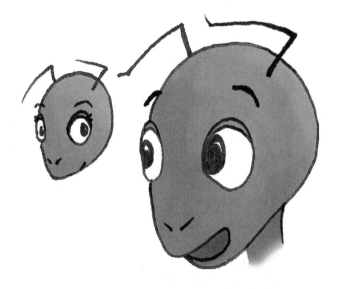

"Should Sam and Sandy trust Drag? Why?"

"¿Deben de confiar en Drag?? ¿Por qué?"

Sam was not sure what to do. This new creature might be their only chance. "Just because this creature is different from us doesn't mean it wants to hurt us!"

Sam no estaba seguro de qué hacer. Esta nueva criatura podría ser su única oportunidad. "El hecho de que esta criatura es diferente de nosotros no quiere decir que quiere hacernos daño!"

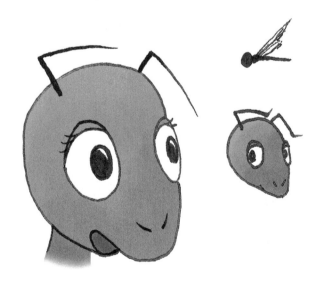

Sam pulled Sandy up as they scrambled from the rock onto the back of Drag, whose strong wings flapped and lifted them into the air.

Sam haló Sandy de la roca hasta la espalda de Drag, y sus alas fuerte batiaron y los levantó en el aire.

As Drag flew, the storm became even stronger and they almost toppled over into the river, which now looked like an ocean!

Mientras Drag voló, la tormenta se hizo aún más fuerte y casi cayeron en el río, que ahora parecía un océano!

As they flew higher into the sky, above the storm, Drag exclaimed "I'm a dragonfly! Welcome to my world, where you can see everything from up high in the sky!"

Mientras volaban alto en el cielo, por encima de la tormenta, Drag exclamó "Soy una libélula! Bienvenido a mi mundo, donde se puede ver todo desde el cielo!"

Sam and Sandy could now see from where the storm had come.

Sam y Sandy ahora podían ver de donde había llegado la tormenta.

"What created the storm? Was it really a storm?"

"¿Que creo la tormenta? ¿Era realmente una tormenta?"

"Thanks, Drag! I'm sorry for not trusting you just because you were different," said Sandy. Sam nodded and said, "Thank you for helping us Drag. What's next?"

"Gracias, Drag! Lo siento por no confiar en ti, sólo porque eres diferente," dijo Sandy. Sam asintió con la cabeza y dijo, "Gracias por ayudarnos Drag. ¿Que sigue?"

"Where did this story take place?"

"¿Cuál es la locación de este cuento?"

Drag smiled and answered, "For now, lets keep flying. I'm sure we'll think of something."

Drag sonrió y respondió: "Por ahora, vamos a seguir volando. Estoy seguro de que ocurrirá algo"

THE END and a beginning
FINAL y principio

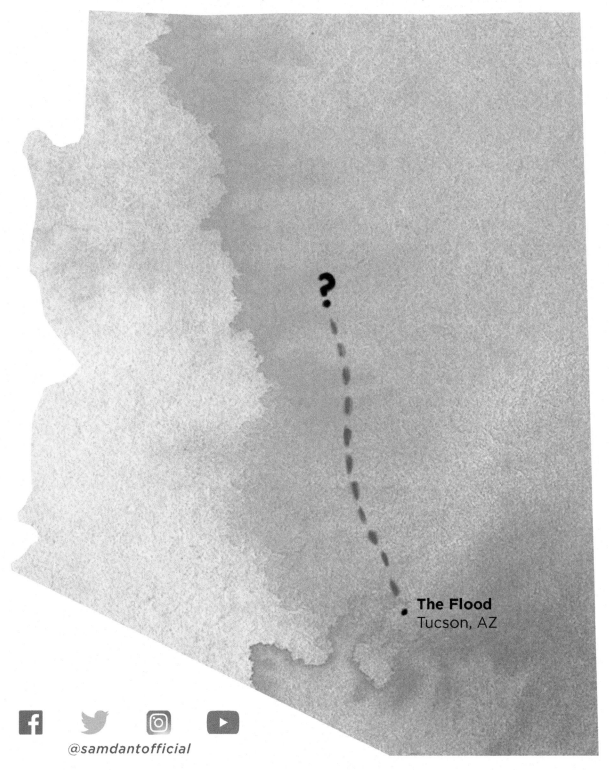

?

The Flood
Tucson, AZ

LEARNING GUIDE

WHAT IS ADVERSITY?

Adversity is something in your life that is a challenge. It could be something unexpected that happens that puts you in a situation where you are uncomfortable. Adversity can be seen as something negative, but it can also be seen as a positive. Many of the greatest human beings have used adversity as a way to grow and improve themselves. In this book, you can point out to your children how Sam, Sandy, and Drag find ways to take adversity (ex. a flood) and learn from the experience.

WHAT IS DIVERSITY AND WHY SHOULD WE EMBRACE IT?

Diversity is about looking at things from different perspectives, becoming comfortable with different ideas, and looking forward to how our differences make our communities interesting and exciting. In this book, Sam and Sandy have to deal with something very different, in the form of Drag the Dragonfly. By embracing Drag, they find a new friend who can help them travel to places that otherwise, they would never have seen.

GUÍA DE APRENDIZAJE

¿QUÉ ES LA ADVERSIDAD?

La adversidad es algo en su vida que es un reto. Podría ser algo inesperado que sucede y te pone en una situación que no es cómoda. Adversidad puede ser vista como algo negativo, pero también como algo positivo. Muchos ser humanos han utilizado la adversidad como una oportunidad para crecer y mejorar. Con este libro, se puede enseñar a sus hijos cómo Sam, Sandy, y Drag encuentran maneras de tomar la adversidad (ej. Una inundación) como una experiencia positiva.

¿QUÉ ES LA DIVERSIDAD Y POR QUÉ DEBEMOS ABRAZARLA?

La diversidad se trata de mirar a las cosas desde perspectivas diferentes, sentirse cómodo con ideas diferentes, y ver cómo nuestras diferencias pueden hacer nuestras comunidades más interesante y emocionante. En este libro, Sam y Sandy tienen que comunicar con algo muy diferente, en forma de Drag, la libélula. Al abrazar Drag, se encuentran con un nuevo amigo que puede ayudarles a viajar a lugares que, de otra forma nunca hubieran visto.

PARENT GUIDE

READING and STORYTELLING WITH YOUR CHILDREN

Reading a story means you read the words in a book to a child. Reading can become boring when the adult reads only the words in the book and when the adult forces a child to sit still and only listen. Storytelling is an adventure! When share a story with a child, you can use a book, and you can read the words in the book, but you also take the time to involve your child in the story. What does that mean?

- When your child asks a question, don't see it as an interruption. See it as a moment to have a conversation with them about what they are noticing in the book.

- When your child wants to move their body, use the strategy known as "embodiment." This is when you become objects, actions and emotions with your body. It's fun for children and it's a great way to help them learn more words. For example, you could ask them what Drag does, and they might say "fly!" At that moment you and your child could use your bodies and pretend to fly. You could then introduce a word that is like flying, such as "hover" and you and your child could pretend to hover with your bodies.

- You can lower and raise the volume of your voice when you read to make it more like a movie, and you can even add music when you read, just like a soundtrack to a movie. Remember, that reading to young children is all about creating a desire to read. You can point out letters and letter sounds, but first connect your child to the idea that storytelling is fun!

GUÍA DE LOS PADRES

CUENTACUENTOS CON SUS HIJOS

Leer un libro significa que usted lee las palabras en un libro a un niño. Esto puede ser aburrido cuando el adulto lee sólo las palabras en el libro y cuando el adulto obliga a un niño a quedarse quieto y sólo escuchar. Contar cuentos es una aventura! Cuando compartimos un cuento con un niño, podemos utilizar un libro, y se puede leer las palabras en el libro, pero también puede tomar el tiempo para involucrar a su hijo en el cuento. ¿Qué significa eso?

- Cuando el niño hace una pregunta, no lo vean como una interrupción. Úselo como un momento para tener una conversación con ellos sobre lo que están notando en el libro.

- Cuando su niño quiere mover su cuerpo, utilice la estrategia conocida como "realización". Esto es cuando se convierte su cuerpo en objetos, acciones y emociones. Es divertido para los niños y es una gran manera de ayudar a aprender más palabras. Por ejemplo, usted podría preguntar que hace la libélula y es posible que el niño contestará "volar!" En ese momento usted y su hijo podrían utilizar sus cuerpos para representar la idea de volar. A continuación, puede introducir una palabra que es como volar, como "flotar" y usted y su hijo podrían "realizar" esa palabra con sus cuerpos.

- Se puede bajar y subir el volumen de su voz cuando se lee para que sea más como una película, e incluso se puede usar música cuando se lee, y así se parece la emocion de una película. Recuerde, que cuando estamos leyendo a los niños pequeños queremos crear un deseo de leer. Se puede señalar las letras y sonidos de las letras, pero primero conecte a los niños a la idea que leer es divertido!

OUR CO-AUTHORS

Sam Feldman is a prolific Artist and National Hispanic Scholar studying Creative Writing and Vocal Studies at the University of Arizona. Having finished her first novel by the age of 12, she is also a performing artist and conductor. Sam is the current musical director of Enharmonics A Cappella, a vocal group which performs on the University of Arizona campus and throughout the Tucson community. Sam also performs with the Tucson Girls Chorus Alumnae, the Helios Ensemble, Audivi Vocem, and the Tucson Symphony Chorus.

Enrique C. Feldman is a world renown educator and performing artist. He is involved in elevating how children learn as the Founder and the Director of Education for the Global Learning Foundation. Enrique is the adaptive editor and Director of Education for Make a Hand, a producer of children's music, a two-time Grammy Nominated Artist, a Redleaf Press Author, and the creator of iBG (Intellectual Brain Games). Additionally, Enrique is the co-creator of the theatrical productions "Dancing in the Universe" and "The Inner Journey."

Abraham Mendoza is an up and coming illustrator who is a designer and illustrator for Art Mine Design in Tucson, Arizona. Having studied graphic design at Pima Community College, Abraham is the illustrator of the children's book "We're all Green on the Inside" by Jenna Stone. He is known for his work in Brand Development, Website UI design, illustrative design, and creative Art direction.

Follow Your Curiosity at www.SamTheAnt.com
for Children's Books, Brainwave Games, and Music!

samtheantofficial@gmail.com

@samdantofficial

Stay Curious

CPSIA information can be obtained
at www.ICGtesting.com
Printed in the USA
LVOW05s1425201016

509595LV00032B/221/P

9 780997 487701